FROGGY
BAKES A CAKE

For Aaron, Paula, Susan, and LouLou,
bakers extraordinaire—J.L.

For Pam Brown, shaker and baker—F.R.

ISBN 0-439-24358-0

Text copyright © 2000 by Jonathan London.
Illustrations copyright © 2000 by Frank Remkiewicz.
All rights reserved.
Published by Scholastic Inc., 555 Broadway, New York, NY 10012,
by arrangement with Penguin Putnam Inc.
SCHOLASTIC and associated logos are trademarks and/or
registered trademarks of Scholastic Inc.

20 19 18 17 16 15 14 13   4 5 6/0

Printed in the U.S.A.   23

First Scholastic printing, January 2001

FROGGY
BAKES A CAKE

By Jonathan London
Illustrated by Frank Remkiewicz

SCHOLASTIC INC.
New York   Toronto   London   Auckland   Sydney
Mexico City   New Delhi   Hong Kong

It was Froggy's mother's birthday.
Froggy was outside making mud pies.

FRROOGGYY! called his father.

"Wha-a-a-at?"
"Help me bake a cake
for your mother!"

"Oh, pleeeaassse," cried Froggy.
"I want to do it all by myself!"
So Froggy flopped
into the kitchen—
flop flop flop.
"You'll need flour,"
said his father.
"And sugar and
chocolate."

"I know!" cried Froggy.
And he pushed his chair against
the counter and climbed up.

He took down the flour.

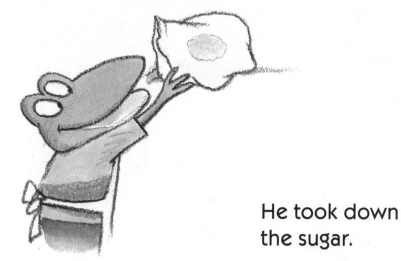

He took down
the sugar.

He took down all
the chocolate candy
his mother had hidden
since Halloween.

"We need *lots* of flour and sugar!" said Froggy. And he dumped a large bag of flour and a whole box of sugar into a big yellow bowl.

"We need *lots* and *lots* of chocolate!" said Froggy. And he dumped in ten handfuls of chocolate-covered flies.

"We need milk, too,"
said Froggy's father.
"I know!" cried Froggy.

And he flopped to the fridge—
flop flop flop— and grabbed
a carton of milk.
"Oops!" It dropped on his foot
and spilled.

"And eggs and butter,"
added his father.
"I know!" cried Froggy.
He snatched a carton of eggs.
"Oops!" He only broke
four or five.

And just one stick of butter
fell on the floor.

"Don't forget the baking
powder," said his father.
"I know!" cried Froggy.
And he climbed up and took
down the baking powder.

Then he cracked seven eggs into the bowl—*crack crack crack crack crack crack crack*—and only a few shells fell in.

And he put in the butter—*blup*—and poured in the milk—*glub glub glub*.

And finally, he dumped in the WHOLE BOX of baking powder—*shloop!*

"Time to mix it all together," said his father.
"I know!" cried Froggy.
And he stirred it and slopped it
and mixed it and plopped it.

Then he dumped all the goopy
cake batter into a cake pan . . .

. . . and shoved the cake into the oven.
And he sang: *"Oogelly boogelly burbly bake.*
I make and I bake
and I wait for the cake!"

FRROOGGYY!

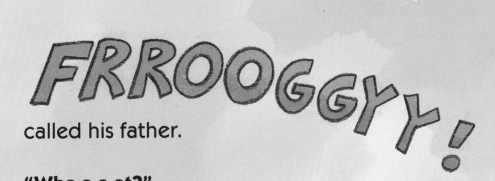

called his father.

"Wha-a-a-at?"
"While you wait for the cake to bake,
help me blow up the balloons."

Froggy helped blow up the balloons.
He blew . . .

and he blew . . .

and he blew and
he blew—*pop!*

"Now," said his father,
"help me set the table."
Froggy helped set the table.
"Oops!" He knocked over the
lemonade and the paper party
tablecloth got all wet.

FRROOGGYY!

called his mother.

"Wha-a-a-at?"
"What smells so good?"

"It's a surprise!" yelled Froggy. And he flopped back to the kitchen—*flop flop flop.*

"Come-and-get-it!" hollered Froggy.
Froggy's mother and father flopped in—
and slid across the buttery floor.
And Froggy said, "Are you ready?"
and opened the oven door.

"Yikes! The cake *exploded!*"
yelped Froggy's father.
"Oops!" cried Froggy, looking
more red in the face than green.
"Too much baking powder, I guess."

"It's good, though," said his father, licking his fingers.

"Wait!" cried Froggy.
"I'll be right back!"—
flop flop flop.

"Happy birthday, Mom!" he said.
And he handed her a fresh
mud pie with a candle in it.
"I made it all by myself!"

"Oh, Froggy," said his mother. "This is the best—uh—birthday pie I ever had."

"What a mess," said Froggy's father.
"Let's go out to celebrate!"
"Great!" said Froggy.
"Yes!" said Froggy's mother.

And together they leap-frogged
all the way to the bakery—
flop flop flop.